Tom and Pippo Make a Mess

PIPPO

HELEN OXENBURY

ALADDIN BOOKS
Macmillan Publishing Company • New York

When Daddy is at home I watch
the way he does things and
I try to do the same thing.

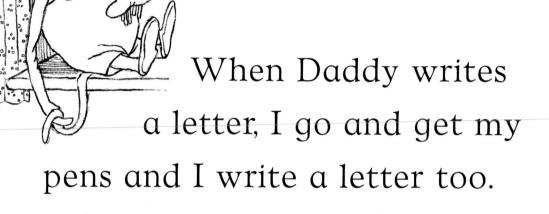

When Daddy writes
a letter, I go and get my
pens and I write a letter too.

When Daddy shaves, I pretend I'm shaving. Pippo thinks I shouldn't waste the shaving cream.

One day Daddy
was doing some
painting. While
he was out of
the room I did some painting to
help him. Daddy said I had
made a mess and
he was angry.

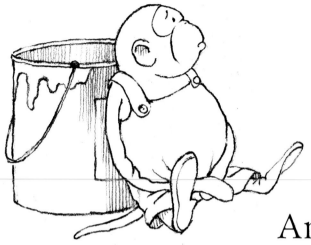

Anyway it was
Pippo who said we should help
Daddy, and I had to be
angry with him.

Daddy says he is going to
work in the garden tomorrow.
I hope he wants me to help.